Messenger
of Fair Island

Messenger
of Fair Island

BY FRANÇOISE de SAINT ANDRÉ *pseud.*

Françoise Jониel

ILLUSTRATIONS BY ANNA ATENE

The John C. Winston Company

Philadelphia • Toronto

To Marie Zara Randall
for her invaluable help and inspiration

Contents

Chapter 1

Important News

"Holà, Michel," called Monsieur Abélard. "You paid me for your bag of caramels, and now you're leaving them on the counter. What are you dreaming about this time, my boy?"

Michel grinned as he came back and picked up the candy he had left next to the storekeeper's elbow.

"I was listening to the drum, Monsieur. There! Don't you hear it? It's telling us that the town crier is on his way. And today, today—"

"Yes, I had forgotten," said the storekeeper. "Today the town crier will have news that you've been waiting to hear for a long time."

Monsieur Abélard folded his clean white apron, covered the caramel jar with its broken top and locked up his moneybox.

"I think I shall go, too," he announced. "But don't wait for me, child. I'm a slow hurrier. And I wouldn't want you to miss the first part of the news."

Usually Michel would have waited for the kindly old storekeeper. But just at that moment—pirouette poof—an extra large puff of excitement sailed into his heart. Then off he scooted down the sandy slope toward his friends.

Half the village must be here, he thought as he finally reached the square and saw the people who had gathered round the town crier. So many fat ones, so many tall ones, standing in the crowd. But Michel did not mind. He had other ways of seeing over the gaily colored wall which rose before him.

Quickly he raced to the old fig tree with his favorite balcony branch. On special occasions such as this, he shared it with Georges and Toto, his two best friends. No one else sat there. It was so high, much too high for the most daring.

"There's Michel," shouted Georges and Toto from the balcony branch. "What kept you? Where have you been?"

"Elevator going up!" cried some of the boys who were sitting closer to the ground.

"Where have I been?" repeated Michel, scrambling into the tree. "Big secret—I've been buying caramels."

As Michel climbed toward the balcony branch, he opened the bag and passed the candy around.

"Merci, Michel, merci!"

Then down below, Michel saw Bébé perched on his father's shoulder. There was one piece of candy left. "Ho there, four-year-old! Ready! Catch!" Then Michel tossed him the paper bag with the last luscious caramel.

"Look, Papa! A candy parachute," exclaimed the little boy, startling the stillness that had finally settled over the square.

The crowd laughed and shuffled about again.

This annoyed the town crier very much.

"Silence!" he commanded, giving his drum a resounding roll. "Do you want to hear the news, or shall I go somewhere else?"

Everyone said SH loudly, softly, then faintly. Softly, then faintly, faintly they said *sh-sh* and looked at the town crier.

Today he seemed different. His face was pink from scrubbing. His hair was combed and parted in a straight line. Today he stood at attention. His carefully polished shoes snapped together like soldiers' boots ready for inspection. And from his bag he pulled a speech written by the Mayor himself.

"Begin, begin!" shouted the crowd.

"Have patience!" answered the town crier, suddenly remembering that he was representing the Mayor. And then because he was representing the Mayor, he cleared his throat in a dignified manner and began.

 4

"Each year at this time, as you all know, we invite a very famous person from the Mainland to be our guest. Since we on our Fair Island of France are well-known for our tropical climate, our beautiful view and, above all for our gay and happy spirit, people usually accept our invitations."

The hurrahs and wild clapping gave the town crier a minute to catch his breath and wipe the perspiration from his glasses.

"Go on. Don't keep us in suspense," shouted Michel and his friends from the fig tree. "Who will it be?"

The town crier wished the Mayor were here. This was all too exciting for him, but he continued reading as well as he could.

"This year we have decided to invite someone you know—someone who has come close to our shores, but who has never visited Fair Island. This year we have decided to invite The Lady with the Golden Voice!"

Michel could hardly keep his balance on the balcony branch. "One of the most famous singers in France!"

How well he remembered one calm lovely evening. Maman and Papa had taken him down through the village, down to the edge of the bay. An excited crowd had gathered there. Suddenly out of the darkness of night came the moon. After the moon, on a barge decorated with flowers, came The Lady with the Golden Voice. Michel never forgot the lovely songs she sang. The beau-

tiful folksongs of France, the merry tunes of village tales, the tender lullabies. How he had wanted her to come to Fair Island to sing them again and again! But when her last clear note had reached the shore, the barge turned toward the North Star, and she sailed away. Away from Fair Island, back to the twinkling lights of the Mainland.

Today the crowd was as excited as Michel.

The Lady with the Golden Voice who had traveled all over the world and sung for kings and queens!

"Hurrah! Bravo!" the people shouted, stamping their feet and clapping long and loud, almost as if she were there.

Suddenly their enthusiasm burned less steadily. Suddenly their excitement flickered like a candle teased by the wind.

Would she come? Would she come back to them?

"I haven't finished," shouted the town crier. "The most important part of the news is yet to come."

The town crier coughed and cleared his throat. It was hard to speak like a mayor, slowly, clearly, in a friendly way, when everyone was chattering so. Still he tried.

"We have heard that this year The Lady with the Golden Voice will sing again to the people of the Mainland. If the skies are clear and the waters calm, she will return to our shores to bring us her encores."

"And when she does?" called out someone.

"Yes, when she does?"

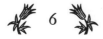

"As soon as her barge is anchored in the bay, we will send out a messenger with our invitation, our invitation to The Lady with the Golden Voice."

"Who? Who?" shouted the boys. "Who? Who?" they shouted as the town crier sat down on his drum and crossed his arms.

"How can I tell you if you scream like owls chasing mice on a moonlight night?" he asked angrily.

A silence filled with curiosity fell over the square and finally allowed the town crier to finish his speech.

"The Mayor has decided that any boy between the ages of twelve and fifteen may participate in a contest to be held here July 19 or shortly thereafter. Definite date to be announced later. The winner will represent the village of Sainte Anne. I have the rules here. Come and get your copies."

"Here! I'll have one. One for me. One for me. Another one over here." The boys spilled out of the tree like soldiers leaping from a camouflage shelter.

"Me too! Me too!" shouted Bébé. "I want the Mayor to give me one, too."

"That's not the Mayor, Monsieur Me Too," laughed Michel. "But wait a minute. I'll get you a blank. Then you can make yourself a paper hat."

"Always helpful Michel," sneered Charles Girard, nudging Michel sharply with his elbow as he went by. "Whatever makes you think the village of Sainte Anne

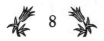 8

would send you as messenger to The Lady with the Golden Voice?"

"I'll be twelve on the day of the contest," answered Michel proudly. "And that's much too old to go about poking people in the ribs with a bony elbow."

"Who's got a bony elbow?" bristled Charles. "Want to fight?"

"I'll fight in the contest," answered Michel. "And I'll fight so hard I'll win."

Charles went away muttering to himself.

"You've got sense, my lad," chuckled an old fisherman who had overheard. "I like a boy who can use his mind and save his muscle for something more important than an argument."

"Thank you, Pépère," answered Michel politely. "But if you'll excuse me now—those contest rules—"

"I know. I know," smiled the old man. "I was in Paris the day she was decorated by the President of France, and I saw her face. It was such a beautiful face!"

Michel raced up to Half Way Point, his favorite stopping place between the village and home. There in a sea of sweet lavender and tender grass he sprawled and dreamed about The Lady with the Golden Voice.

I'll tell her about our little town. The lovely things about our town. How rays of morning sun slide off the red-tiled roofs and paint our stucco walls all pink and gold. And then she'll come!

I'll tell her how our white-sailed ships play games with the sea and race with the tides in frostiness of dawn. Then she'll come—The Lady with the Golden Voice.

"Michel, Michel!" His name came hurtling down into the midst of sweet lavender and tender grass, into the very midst of his dreams. "Hurry! Hurry! It's almost suppertime, and we need water from the spring."

Michel folded the contest rules. After supper, he thought with a sigh.

Maman waved to Michel as he trudged up the rest of the hill. Her reminder was a cheerful one. "Chéri, you forgot to fill the water jug, and Papa will soon be home."

Every evening Michel took the shortcut to the spring. Sliding down a sand dune, sliding down a narrow trail covered with slippery pine needles. That was his path to the spring. But tonight he took the long way round and dreamed.

Fill your ears with the laughter of the tides and the songs of the birds, whispered his heart. Fill your eyes with sleepy clouds and pink and purple patterns that are sky. And remember them. Remember them for The Lady with the Golden Voice.

During supper Michel was very quiet. Papa talked about the crops and the fruit trees in the orchard. "We need rain," said Monsieur Dupont gloomily. "Lots of rain and soon."

"It can rain all it wants to until her visit. But on that

 10

special day not a drop," exclaimed Michel suddenly. "Rain is ugly as it falls into the gray-green sea."

"What do you mean, chéri?" asked Maman gently.

Then Michel told Papa and Maman about the possible coming of The Lady with the Golden Voice.

"I see," said Papa, stuffing his pipe with tobacco. "You want our island to be beautiful when she comes."

"If she comes," said Maman, starting to clear the table. "You know she is a very famous singer. She may not have time for us."

Michel was not listening. He had started to read the rules of the contest. Slowly and carefully he read.

CONTEST RULES

1. *The contest will take place July 19 or shortly thereafter.*
2. *Each contestant must be a resident of Sainte Anne.*
3. *He must not be younger than twelve, and not older than fifteen.*
4. *He must be strong and brave.*

Michel stopped reading a minute. "Do you think I am strong and brave, Papa?"

Monsieur Dupont thought before answering. "You have never been put to a real test, my son. But I believe that you are strong and unafraid."

Michel seemed satisfied with the answer.

"Rule number five," he announced, giving his glass a jolly ring with the side of his knife before starting.

11

5. On the day of the contest, each contestant must be able to ride a bicycle from the Village Square up Saint Christopher Hill and back to the Village Square in not more than two hours.
6. Finally, between now and the contest date, he must prepare an invitation to The Lady with the Golden Voice, and after the race recite it to the Mayor, the judges, and all who may wish to hear.

"You see, Maman. It is not too difficult. And I shall try so hard that I will surely win."

"You have never written a speech, Michel. How will you ever think of what to say?"

"The words are in my heart, Maman. I shall listen to them speak."

"And the bicycle, Michel. You have none. I shall not be able to afford a new one until the crops are sold.

"How will you ever ride up Saint Christopher Hill?"

"If only Monsieur Hugo hadn't backed his hay wagon into your bicycle," mourned Michel. "But perhaps I can borrow one. Tomorrow I shall try."

The brightness that had returned into Michel's voice reminded Maman that it was time to brighten up the room.

"Papa, a match please," she said, removing the glass chimney from the oil lamp that stood proudly in the center of the kitchen table. "I cleaned the wicks today. Voilà! Presto! We shall have some light."

But a cool evening breeze made the oil lamps flicker like fireflies.

Michel went to the window to close the blinds. Below him stood Charles Girard, listening.

"Just wanted to see if you were going to enter the contest, now that you've read the rules," he said with a crooked smile.

"Why not?" retorted Michel, winking at the stars.

"What about rule number five?" teased Charles. "How will you get up Saint Christopher Hill? You have no bike. You broke your father's, you know!"

"That's not true," blazed Michel.

"The blinds, Michel. Please close them, dear. Papa can't read by the light of the moon."

Michel closed the blinds with a bang and ran into the garden. He had refrained from fighting once today. But now—now. He clenched his fists. What had Charles meant by telling lies like these?

Puzzled and angry, he questioned the air where Charles had stood. But Charles had gone. Charles with the crooked smile had vanished into the night.

Chapter 2

An Important Question

Michel Dupont had no alarm clock. He did not need one, for every morning at the same time an excited little breeze skipped over the sea to Fair Island, blowing off its blanket of sleep. Wake up, it whispered to the mimosa trees. Wake up, it whispered to the sheep and the lambs in the fields. Wake up, Michel, it whispered, too.

At the sound of mimosa trees stirring and stretching their arms, Michel would open his eyes. Just in time to see a trail of night gliding off the walls of his room, running away from the sun. Shadows running away from the sun, that was the beginning of another day. A new day filled with excitement.

As Michel slipped into a striped shirt and dark-blue

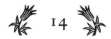 14

shorts and tightened the buckles on his brown sandals, the words Christopher Hill kept turning round and round in his mind. Christopher Hill, Christopher Hill, like the wheels of a bicycle—the bicycle he had to borrow to be in the contest.

I must find one today, he thought, jumping the stairs three at a time on his way to breakfast.

"Bonjour, Papa—Maman. Mmmm, that strawberry jam looks good!"

Maman had already set the table on a gay red and white checkerboard tablecloth. Now she was pouring some café au lait into Michel's blue bowl. Papa was cutting three thick slices of bread from a large crusty loaf as long as a baseball bat.

"Bonjour, mon p'tit."

"Bonjour, chéri."

Maman's smile was cheerful and welcoming, like the good breakfast on the gay red and white cloth, but Papa looked worried. He didn't say much during breakfast. After every sip of coffee he would turn his head toward the window, searching the clouds for rain. Every once in a while his dark-brown fingers would drum funny little trills on the table as if he were trying to hurry the rain that was so slow in coming. Finally, when he got up from his place, he looked at Michel as if to say, Sorry, son. I know you have other plans. But there's work to be done.

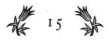

Then he spoke out loud. "No weeds to pull today. Still we must water the beans and tomatoes this morning, or next month we shall be sitting before an empty dinner table."

"I'm coming right away, Papa," answered Michel with a wink for Maman and a last lick of strawberry jam on his fingers.

Michel didn't mind watering the garden, even if it was hard work. He was proud of the fine plants that he and Papa cared for, and he wanted to help them live.

As he and Papa hurried toward the garden, Michel talked of other years. Of times when there had been a specially good crop. Of times when Papa had sold all his best vegetables to Monsieur Gabriel, who owned the small hotel in the village.

"Do you remember how I used to ask him if his guests had liked your vegetables and whether they had taken second helpings of your tomatoes and string beans?"

Papa smiled and imitated the innkeeper's funny answers. Nodding and winking, he described his words with excited gestures, just like Monsieur Gabriel—"Oui, oui, oui, mon garçon! Of all the légumes I bought last week, your papa's were the freshest, the tastiest. Why, little Adèle from Bordeaux has grown three inches since she's been eating them. And poor skinny little Gaston from Paris has gained five pounds on those tomatoes and string beans."

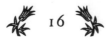 16

Then Papa became serious again. "No one could get fat on this year's crop," he sighed, showing his dry garden. "And look! Something has been nibbling again." He stooped over his plants and examined them carefully. "It can't be bugs or insects this time," he said. "They make lace doilies out of my lettuce when they settle on its leaves. It must be that scamp of a rabbit. Though he has been afraid to come back since you—"

"Oh, I see why!" exclaimed Michel, suddenly pointing to a huddled heap at the end of a row. "Madame Gypsy Scareaway has fallen down on the job this time!"

Michel ran to pick her up. "Poor Madame Gypsy. You've had a bad fall," he said consolingly. "But that's all right. You're not like Humpty Dumpty. I can easily put you together again." Before Papa could say, "Too bad, c'est dommage," Madame Gypsy was once more her own Scareaway self.

Michel and Toto had made her out of an old weather-beaten mop. They had thrust the handle deep into the ground. On this they nailed a crosspiece of wood for arms. They had dressed her in a white blouse and a brilliant red skirt and had tied a handkerchief of gay colors around her straggles of uncombed hair. Later Michel had another idea. He had sewed four large earrings to her bright kerchief. Every time the wind puffed a bit, the earrings clanged a warning to all unwanted animal visitors—Madame Scareaway is standing guard!

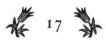

"There now," said Michel. "Stand up as tall and straight as you can, and keep that nibbling old scamp out of the garden. I've got a job to do, too."

Quickly he raced toward the center of the garden. Quickly he unhooked his twin buckets from the side of the tool shed and lowered them clanging into the deepness of the well. Just like a game, he thought, filling the buckets to the top with cool, clear water and bringing them up—first one, then the other, without spilling a drop.

Bush after bush. Plant after plant. Row after row, he watered, racing against time. By nine o'clock it would be too late to continue, for then the sun's hot rays would bake the dampened soil into a hard cake of earth. "Earth around plants should be worked into light crumbly soil," Papa always said.

All at once Michel shouted, "I must be getting strong, Papa. These buckets of water no longer hurt my back or make my arms and legs feel stiff and sore."

"Stronger for that contest!" laughed Papa.

Michel was pleased, pleased to hear Papa laughing again and pleased to be stronger for the contest.

By ten o'clock Michel had finished loosening the earth around the watered plants. By ten-thirty he was at Half Way Point, greeting the village in the valley below.

A comfortable feeling crept into Michel's heart as he counted the never-changing buildings spread out be-

18

fore him like a miniature town under a Christmas tree—
the church, the school, the town hall, and all the little
shops gathered together in friendly fashion around the
parklike square.

Splashes of colored scarfs and skirts darting about like
restless balloons on Carnival Day told Michel the village
was now wide-awake.

There's Jacques. Or is it Pierre? Or Paul? Michel tried

to recognize his friends and then gave up. People are all the same from a distance, he thought. You have to get close to them to know what they're really like. And away he flew down the steep slope.

Suddenly Michel jumped. Something moving about in the bushes startled him. Could it be a snake, coiled and ready to strike? His mind and feet moved quickly as he grabbed a heavy stick. Then slowly he crept toward the stirring clump of bushes, watching every blade of grass, watching for that small snake with its dangerous poisonous bite. Michel beat the grass ahead of him, getting closer and closer to the trembling bush.

All at once the bush began to talk. "Don't hit us. Don't hit us, Michel!" And out popped Georges and Toto, looking very much embarrassed.

When he saw their faces, Michel wondered for a moment if his friends had been hiding in fun or on purpose. But he didn't think about that for very long.

"Toto, you're just the one I wanted to see," he exclaimed.

Toto didn't give Michel a chance to continue. "Listen to this," he interrupted, mysteriously unfolding a piece of paper covered with artistic flourishes of purple ink. "It's from Oncle Dominique, and this is what it says:

> Cher Toto:
> When the *Silver Queen* docks at Fair Island next week, she will bring you a birthday present from me. He is white and black and the friendliest puppy I have ever seen. Feed him well, and love him dearly.
> Your affectionate
Oncle Dominique

"You're lucky," laughed Michel. "What will you call him?"

"Frisk," said Toto quietly as he began to whistle a gay little tune.

Michel smiled. He could almost see Toto's birthday present trotting beside them, a jolly, frolicky puppy with a short wagging tail, a turned-up nose and flippy-floppy ears. Toto could make you see anything when he whistled.

"Bravo," cheered Michel. "But don't forget I have a question to ask you. I was wondering if—"

This time Georges interrupted. "Papa told me to ask you if you could help us in the vineyards this summer. At the end of August we'll need some good grape pickers."

Last year George's father had given Michel a small share of the crop with permission to taste while he was picking. That was the best part of the bargain, thought Michel. Tasting while picking, cooling his dry mouth with the sweet, fresh juice of ripened grapes.

"I'll come," answered Michel happily. "Tell your papa to have his picking baskets ready. I shall be bright and early. Earlier than Red Rooster, who thinks that he can waken the sun." Michel tried to make Georges and Toto smile. They were so serious today.

But Georges and Toto did not smile. They talked on and on. They talked about almost everything that had ever happened on Fair Island. They talked about school and the new boy from the Mainland. They discussed hunting and fishing and sailing. And, like their fathers, they wondered why the government had never brought electricity or running water to the island.

"Papa doesn't think it could make us much happier," said Michel. "He says real happiness comes from kind thoughts and brave deeds, not from things."

As the three boys reached the bottom of the hill, Georges told Michel they were going to take a shortcut to the bakery.

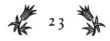

"Not before I ask you my question," Michel almost shouted.

Toto moved on hurriedly, but Michel grabbed his shoulders and yanked him back.

"What's the matter, Toto? Why are you running away? I only wanted to ask you if I could borrow your bike for the contest."

Toto pushed Michel away more roughly than he intended. "I can't lend you my bike," he muttered. "Charles Girard said you broke your father's, and if anything should happen to mine—"

Michel's dark eyes lowered with disappointment. "I thought you were my friend," he said sadly. "You know very well that Monsieur Hugo backed his hay wagon into my father's bike."

Georges tried to be helpful. "You could have mine, but I'll be using it in the contest." Michel turned away. How could Toto, his best friend, believe what Charles Girard had told him?

Michel had never felt like this before. His cheeks burned as much as if Toto had slapped them. Now he realized he could no longer trust his friend. I've lost something, he thought. I've lost something. It was so important.

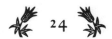

Chapter 3

Fishing for a Bicycle

Michel walked on slowly in silence, as silent as the tall, straight cypress trees that lined the roads of Fair Island.

I shall have to forget my speech to The Lady with the Golden Voice, he thought. No one will ever lend me a bicycle now.

Angrily he scuffed his brown sandals against the stony path curving around the church. Angrily the pebbles flew before him, stampeding and stirring up the dust. Michel gave them another disappointed kick, tumbling them over the grassy bank of the rectory, straight into the garden where Father Francis was feeding the birds.

Father Francis looked up. "Good boy," he called out, tossing one last golden spray of crumbs to the birds. "I'm

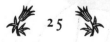

glad to see you saying your prayers—a little late in the morning perhaps, though talking with God at any time is an excellent habit to cultivate."

Michel's tanned face grew red with embarrassment.

"Father. Mon père," he stammered. "I was speaking, it is true, but my words were not those of a prayer."

Michel was sorry to have hurt kind Father Francis, but it wasn't fair to pretend.

"I like your honesty, my boy," answered Father Francis, looking closely at Michel. "But what is worrying you, my son? Come tell me about it!"

Michel didn't quite know where to begin. "Father, have you ever dreamed of doing something exciting?"

"Yes, my son, often."

"Then you will understand how much I want to take part in the contest we heard about the other day. If I win, I will be Messenger of Fair Island, Messenger to The Lady with the Golden Voice. You've heard of her, haven't you? She's sung before kings and queens and has traveled all over the world!"

Father Francis nodded. "God has given her a wonderful gift. I hope she will come to share it with us," he answered, picking a few figs for Michel from the great, green umbrella-like tree which changed one corner of his garden into a cool carpet of shade.

"Thank you, mon père. My favorite fruit!"

Michel peeled the figs quickly, exclaiming "Comme c'est bon!" each time he popped one into his mouth.

But Father Francis was not yet satisfied. The troubled, anxious look hadn't disappeared from the boy's eyes.

"It's the bicycle," Michel burst out suddenly. "I need one for the contest. And Papa can't afford a new one."

"Anyone in the village will be glad to lend you a bike, Michel. Haven't you asked?"

"It's not that easy, mon père. Charles Girard came to my house last night and said he knew I had bumped into Monsieur Hugo's hay wagon. That's all wrong. It was Monsieur Hugo who bumped into me. Now Charles will spread this story throughout the village, and no one will trust me any more."

"People are quick to believe false tales," answered the

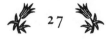

priest sadly. "But perhaps you are imagining things. Perhaps Charles was trying to frighten you. What does Monsieur Hugo say?"

"He just shrugs his shoulders and says, 'Bicycles and hay wagons were never meant to be friends.' "

"Mon père! Mon père!" An excited voice cut shrill patterns of sound in the morning air. It was Jeanette, the cook, calling from the kitchen window. "Little Paul is here. His father has been hurt in an accident and wants to see you right away."

Father Francis turned to Michel. "I would gladly promise my bike," he said. "But you see, I might have to leave at the very moment you would want to use it. Go into the village. There will be many who will want to help you."

A few minutes later, as Michel crossed the square, he remembered he hadn't thanked Father Francis for his kindness. Michel felt sorry. Why had he forgotten? Father Francis had always been so good to him.

"Sorry, sorry, sorry," clucked Madame Mirabelle's parrot as she sunned herself in front of the bakery shop.

Could she be speaking to me? thought Michel as he reached for the crisp sunflower seeds he always carried in his pocket for Josette.

"You don't deserve one," he laughed. "But maybe you are hungry. Come on, have one instead of making unkind remarks about people."

Josette stopped ruffling her feathers and made pleasant cooing sounds like a dove.

"Nice boy. Nice nice boy!" she raved.

Michel gave Josette all the seeds he had in his pocket.

"Nice nice boy," she jabbered.

"Josette, don't annoy the customers!" called Madame Mirabelle through the open door. "Oh, it's you, Michel! Come in and rest yourself before you walk home."

"Thank you very much, Madame," Michel spoke gratefully. "I'll stop in on my way back. Now I'm going down to the dock."

"Fish, fish, fish!" chuckled Josette.

"You can't guess what I'm going to catch," said Michel, tweaking one of Josette's loose feathers. "I'm going fishing for a bicycle."

"Awk!" screamed Josette. "Bicycle? Bicycle?" She rolled her eyes and stared at Monsieur Me Too, who had stopped to look at cherry tarts and peach squares in the bakery window.

"Let me go with you. Take me fishing for a bicycle, too," begged little four-year-old, to whom a bicycle sounded even more exciting than a peach pie or a cherry tart.

"Where's your mother? Ask her if she'll let you go."

Monsieur Me Too skipped into the post office. Michel heard a disappointed wail, then a short happy laugh.

"Non non non! Oui oui oui!" chuckled Josette.

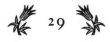

"You'll have to be very good," warned Michel when the little boy came out.

Me Too took Michel's hand and promised to be very good.

"Good good good!" screamed Josette until the tall boy and the little boy had disappeared into the soft shadows of the trees bordering the dusty road.

As they hurried on, the Mediterranean spread out her deepest blue mantle for them to see. Glad little waves curtsied and bowed in happy welcome.

"She is kind now," said Michel. "That is the Mediterranean, kind one day and cruel the next."

Monsieur Me Too wasn't listening to Michel. "There is Pépère on the dock," he shouted, waving to the old fisherman. "Let's go see what he's doing."

Pépère was sewing a piece of cloth on the torn right-hand corner of his sail. As he stopped to rethread his huge needle, he saw Michel and four-year-old.

"Soon she'll be racing the tides in frostiness of dawn!" he said proudly.

Michel admired the fisherman's work. "How did it happen, Pépère?" he asked.

Me Too sat down and unwound some thread for Pépère's next needleful, while the old man filled his cheeks full of air. Then, like a sly goblin playing tricks with a bag of wind, he let the air out with a roar.

Me Too jumped as if a balloon had popped.

 30

"Sounds like a tornado," laughed Michel.

"That's just what it was!" chuckled Pépère. "That's what the wind did to my sail. Blew a hole right through it."

"Please do it again, Pépère. Again," begged Me Too, who couldn't stop laughing.

While Pépère entertained Me Too, Michel crossed over to the other side of the dock. He watched as another fisherman was getting ready to paint the sides of his boat.

"The waves were so rough between here and the Mainland last Friday they scraped all the paint off," he said grumpily. "And I've got other things to do besides paint," he added.

Michel jumped at his chance. "I'll do the job for you if you lend me your bicycle for the contest next week," he offered hopefully.

"That's a bargain," answered the fisherman. "I've got nets to mend. Can you take over now?"

Michel called Me Too. "Come on, Bébé. You can help me paint."

But Me Too was listening to a sea story that Pépère was telling with rolling eyes and excited gestures. So he shook his head non non non.

"I'll watch him," said Pépère. "He'll be all right."

Michel dipped his brush into the gray paint. "I've caught my bicycle this time," he said happily. And all his happiness went into his work.

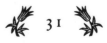

"Listen to the slap-slap of the water against the dock," said Me Too suddenly. "The waves are clapping for you, Michel."

Michel had almost finished. He stopped painting and looked up. Bébé was coming toward him.

Michel jumped up and went to the little boy, holding out his hand to show him the way. But Bébé paid no attention to Michel's hand. He followed his own path, hurrying toward the gleam of the paint can and the bright shiny surface of the boat.

"Not that way. It's too close to the edge."

Michel's warning came too late. Bébé was skidding over a mat of slimy seaweed which a rising tide had thrown over the side of the pier.

Michel shouted for help and grabbed for Bébé's belt, but his fingers clutched only a handful of air. Bébé was already over the side.

He had gone down when Michel reached the water—down, down through a scum of foam.

Michel heard a life preserver spank the water beside him, but it was of no use to him yet. Down, down he went through dense, dark, flowing shadows, through sharp currents jabbing icily at his sides. Down, down he swam, forcing himself to forget the pain in his chest and the pounding in his head, remembering only to keep his eyes open for Bébé.

At last he saw little four-year-old, his belt caught on

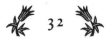

32

a nail at the bottom of the pier. "If I take time to go up for air, it will be too late. Bébé will never say 'Me Too' again."

Michel forgot the pain in his chest and the stiffness in his arms. He swam downward with all his strength, kicking all thoughts of safety into a churning swirl behind him.

Bébé seemed hours away from his grasp. But Michel finally caught hold of the nail and tugged at Bébé's belt with all his might. Bébé's belt was held fast.

Michel heard a buzzing in his ears. The buzzing seemed to turn into words—into the voice of Father Francis. "Pray, my son, and God will give you strength."

Michel's prayer was the shortest he ever said. "One more second," he begged with all his heart and soul.

In that second he whipped out his knife and slashed the belt.

Little Me Too was free at last.

Up, up through icy streams and foamy scum they flew. Up to the life preserver that waited on the waves. Up to a rim of faces and outstretched arms. Michel lifted Bébé to those who would give him artificial respiration and make him breathe again. Then he fell back into the water.

Foamy scum . . . Pépère's anxious face . . . Toto . . . little Monsieur Me Too . . . bicycles on the end of fishhooks . . . and The Lady with the Golden Voice—all

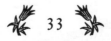 33

passed in front of Michel's eyes as he fell back exhausted beneath the surface of the water.

Fifteen long minutes passed before Doctor Martin cleared his throat and said, "I think he's breathing normally again. Don't crowd around the boy. He needs all the air he can get."

A loud AH of relief finished waking Michel. His head felt light—light as a feather drifting, drifting into the deep blue of the sea. He fought against drifting and thought about his arms and legs. They were like heavy

weights dragging him down, down. He fought against sinking and thought about Bébé. He tried to get to his feet, but Doctor Martin laid a gentle hand on his shoulder. "Rest a few more minutes, mon garçon," he said quietly.

Michel looked up. Round faces, thin faces, upside-down faces. Never had he seen so many people gathered in one small spot. "I'm all right." He tried to sound cheerful.

"Move back, or I shall send you all away," ordered Doctor Martin.

There was Father Francis smiling proudly.

"Those figs gave me the strength," Michel said.

"And God the courage," nodded Father Francis.

Everyone pressed closer to Michel again, forgetting all about the doctor's warning.

"If my little boy had not been so stubborn, this would never have happened," sobbed a pretty young woman in a yellow dress.

"Why is she crying?" asked Michel, his heart pounding at the thought of her answer. "Where is Bébé? Didn't he—?"

"Bébé's mother is weeping because she has been very much upset," said Doctor Martin. "But she is deeply grateful, Michel."

"Me Too, Me Too," chirped Bébé. "Me Too is grateful."

Michel sank back on the pier, and just before he re-

laxed in a deep, comfortable sleep, he caught sight of Georges and Toto.

"It's Toto who went in after you," said Doctor Martin. "He brought you back up."

"I'll put your name on my bike for the Contest Day," grinned Toto, who seemed to be whispering. But Michel heard it all. And as he slept he smiled.

Chapter 4

Waiting for the Silver Queen

Pink and purple patterns of sky floated lazily on the pail of water Michel set down by the kitchen door.

"Maman, your bucket is full," he called gaily. "Did you find many flowers?"

"In here, chéri. I think I have picked as many as last week."

"Oh! Even more and prettier ones!" exclaimed Michel, admiring the rainbow-colored bouquets Madame Dupont was preparing to take down to the Village Square. "I know the tourists will buy them all."

Today was Friday, Visitors' Day, the day tourists from all over the world gathered on the docks at Toulon and climbed aboard the *Silver Queen*. Travelers from Italy, England, and America, crossing a patch of sea to

discover the loveliness of Fair Island. The loveliness of which Papa, Maman, Michel and all their friends were so proud.

Papa, who had been packing peaches in two large baskets, stopped a minute to look at the flowers.

"They are very beautiful indeed!" he said, choosing a pretty bloom and pinning it to Maman's dress. "Your mother is a wonderful person." He bowed. "Like a magician who pulls rabbits out of the strangest places, she makes these blossoms appear. Where do they come from? Tell us your secret, Maman."

"A magician never reveals his tricks," replied Maman. "Ask the flowers. Perhaps they will tell you how I came upon them."

As Maman teased, she whirled about the kitchen in the colorful costume of Provence that she always wore on Visitors' Day, twirling in gay circles, trying to shake out one tiny wrinkle from her long red and white striped skirt.

"Careless irons," she scolded smilingly. "Naughty irons! You forgot one wrinkle—one tiny wrinkle!"

"Don't make them angry," warned Papa jokingly. "Next time you press my coat they will get too hot and burn a hole in my sleeve. And then I will have no costume for Visitors' Day."

Michel loved Visitors' Day, when the Market Square seemed to turn into a stage, when all the people of Sainte

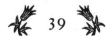

Anne dressed up and had a part to play. Showing, selling, singing, dancing, dressed in the costumes of Provence—all had a part in the play, Maman the prettiest and Papa the handsomest of course.

Michel studied their reflections in the shiny copper pans hanging over the stove. Wouldn't it be fun to take a piece of charcoal and sketch their outlines on the bottom of the pans?

But the crazy cuckoo bird in the old cuckoo clock on the wall had other plans. Hurry, my good family, hurry,

hurry, it seemed to say as it whirred and clattered with
excitement in its telling of the time.

"Yes, we'd better hurry," repeated Papa in a calmer
way. "The *Silver Queen* and her tourists will come and
go before we reach the Village Square, and the peaches
in my baskets will be wasted."

Papa looked at Michel and wondered. Almost a week
had passed since Michel had saved Monsieur Me Too.
His face was still pale and his shoulders not so straight.

"How do you feel now, my boy? Strong enough to

help your mother with the bucket of water for her flowers? Remember the doctor told you not to do too much after your skirmish with the sea."

There was laughter in Michel's dark eyes as he snapped to attention.

"As long as it turned out all right, I think deep-sea diving agrees with me," he saluted.

Suddenly Michel relaxed. "Sh!" he whispered, pointing to the bucket outside the door. Two strange-looking birds were balancing themselves on its rim.

"Please don't scare them," begged Michel. "They won't drink it all."

"Aha!" smiled Maman, gathering her bouquets from the table. "On Fair Island when an unknown bird eats or drinks at your door, they say a visitor is coming."

"A visitor! Do you think . . .? Could it be . . .?" Michel's words tripped over each other with excitement. "The Lady with the Golden Voice?"

"Not necessarily The Lady with the Golden Voice, my son. And look, your animated gestures have frightened the birds away."

Sadly Michel watched an upward fluttering of blue and gold—a graceful dip—a speck in the patterns of sky.

All the way down to Half Way Point he wondered about The Lady with the Golden Voice. Did those strange birds really foretell her coming? Or did their sudden flying away mean that she would not come at all?

Were these signs true? Or were they stories people liked to believe?

Stories, stories, stories, hummed the locusts, singing their summer songs.

Who knows? Who knows? whispered the breeze sweeping through the fields at Half Way Point. Fields purple with lavender. Purple and lavender, colors of mystery.

At Half Way Point, Maman made Michel sit down a few minutes. The bucket of water was heavy, and Michel still looked tired.

Papa stopped, too. His baskets of peaches had rubbed sore spots on his shoulders under his coat. "Three peaches less should lighten my load," he laughed. "One for you, one for you, and one for me."

As Michel bit into cool mellow sweetness, his gaze skipped across the rooftops of Sainte Anne and out to sea like a telescope searching. "No *Silver Queen* yet," he announced. "She's always late, it seems."

"Perhaps she's waiting while someone has gone to remind the Mayor that the ship cannot sail without his weekly message to the people of Fair Island. Such a good man, our Mayor. But so forgetful," sighed Maman.

"Oh! I hope if he can't be here today, he remembers to send his announcement about the contest date," exclaimed Michel. "All we know is that it's to take place some day during the week of July nineteenth."

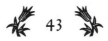 43

At the thought of the contest, Michel felt strong again. "I could carry one of your baskets of peaches, Papa," he called, jumping to his feet.

From the quietness of Half Way Point into busy Sainte Anne they came, bringing with them their thoughts and dreams and the fragrance of flowers.

As they neared the rectory garden, Father Francis waved. "Feeling quite sturdy, my boy?"

44

"Oh! Oui, mon père."

Maman chose a bouquet of pink and blue flowers. Papa picked out his largest peaches.

"For you, mon père," they offered.

"Merci, my good people. Your kindness is reflected in the beauty of these lovely gifts," he said gratefully. "By the way, Michel, when is the contest to be?"

"I hope we find out today," answered Michel.

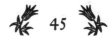

45

"I hope, I hope, I hope," Michel repeated in a sing-songy marching tune until he had reached the Market Square. Then he walked more slowly as Maman cleared a path for him—up a lane of tables, through a passageway of stands.

Carefully, carefully Michel carried Maman's flowers in their pail of water, calling to his friends as he went by.

"Why is the *Queen* so late?"

"Soon did you say?"

"How many visitors do they expect?"

"Oh, more than that!"

"I hope some stay awhile. It's fun to have them at the inn."

Some visitors stayed a week or two, a month or so. But most returned to the Mainland in the evening, with flowers, a bit of lace, a coral necklace and the laughter of Fair Island in their hearts.

Suddenly Michel left Maman's table.

Louder than the scorekeeping of men at their games, louder than the accordion, the fiddle and the clarinet came the voice of Josette.

"Awk awk awk!" she shrieked. "Let me go."

Quickly Michel skipped through the lanes of tables. Quickly he ran toward Madame Mirabelle's shop. Some-one was bothering Josette. Someone was hurting her.

"Let that parrot alone," he stormed. "Josette doesn't belong to you."

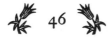

46

It was Charles Girard again. He seemed annoyed. He didn't want to make a scene in front of everyone.

"I wasn't doing anything," he sulked, stuffing a few red and green feathers in his pocket. "Josette's been bad, and she's supposed to be punished. Look, Madame Mirabelle has tacked a sign under Josette's stand:

DO NOT GIVE ANY GOODIES TO JOSETTE. IN FACT PLEASE DO NOT SPEAK TO HER. SHE HAS BEEN VERY NAUGHTY. TODAY SHE PUT HER FOOT IN ONE OF MY APPLE TARTS AND PECKED HOLES IN MY PEACH PIE.

Michel burst out laughing. "Josette, why did you do such a thing? No sunflower seeds for you, my dear!"

"Nice boy. Nice boy. Nice boy," cooed Josette. Jumping on Michel's shoulder, she rubbed her feathery face against his cheek, hoping he would change his mind.

"No, Josette. You can't coax me that way. I must obey Madame Mirabelle's sign. Get down, you silly bird."

"Awk!" sputtered Josette, not insisting. Pretending not to care, she jumped back on her stand and turned toward the men and boys who were bowling.

Bowling was a favorite pastime for men and boys in southern France. They bowled at lunch time and after supper and on Sunday afternoons. In sandy squares or on cool green grass wherever they happened to be.

"Come on, Michel, we need an extra player. Jacques

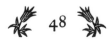 48

Durand has gone down to the dock to see if the *Silver Queen* is stuck on a sandbar. She's so very late today."

Monsieur Me Too, who was watching the game, ran out upon the green and started to pick up the smallest ball. "For you, Michel," he called.

"No no!" shouted the men half angrily. "Don't move the ball, Bébé. It must not be changed an inch. Not half an inch. Each player tries to roll his ball as close to the little one as he can."

Somebody brought Michel a big ball.

"Go on, lad. See what you can do," called the town crier. He too was waiting for the *Silver Queen*, which he hoped would bring the Mayor's message from the Mainland.

Grasping his ball, Michel sent it spinning across the green. Bouncing, rolling, racing across the green it sped. But not so far as usual. Not to the spot which Michel had made up his mind to reach.

"Still tired," snickered Charles Girard. "Christopher Hill may be too steep for you."

"I don't use my arms for pedaling," retorted Michel. "Do you?"

Charles Girard opened his mouth to speak. Instead of his words, Michel heard the solemn horn of the *Silver Queen*. Make way for Her Majesty! it seemed to say.

"Beat you!" Michel teased, as he and Charles hopped over the balls and dashed down toward the dock.

Chapter 5

*The Winds
Grow Cold*

Side by side toward the dock they flew. Michel
sped ahead. Then Charles.

"I can't pick a winner," announced Pépère, pulling in
his nets. "It's a tie!"

I'll have to do better than that on the day of the contest, thought Michel as he helped Pépère dump his sleek,
shiny, flopping fish into a great tub of water.

"Here she is," yelled the men and boys who had come
down to greet the *Silver Queen.*

Around the tip end of the island she appeared with
quiet dignity. Down a corridor of blue in stately majesty
she sailed, nodding her thanks. Nodding to the fishing
boats which fluttered their sails in welcome. Welcome,
welcome, welcome!

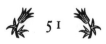

Handkerchiefs on the pier also waved with welcome.

There were Monsieur Abélard and his helper waiting for their shipment of nails. There were the innkeeper and the town crier. There were Father Francis and Doctor Martin and Michel and Georges and Toto. Everyone cheered as the *Silver Queen* edged up to the pier. Everyone cheered as ropes whirled through the air and the gangplank was secured to the dock.

"Where's Toto?" shouted a sailor. "I've got something for him."

"Throw it down," called Charles.

"Can't be done," answered the sailor sharply. "This object is fragile." In his hand he held a puppy. A jolly frolicky-looking puppy with a short wagging tail, a turned-up nose and flippy-floppy ears.

It was Frisk.

Toto whistled a cute little tune. Come stay with me, and let's be friends, it seemed to say.

Frisk pricked up his flippy-floppy ears, gave an approving bark and jumped right off the sailor's hand into

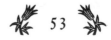

53

Toto's outstretched arms. "Love him dearly," Oncle Dominique had said. And from that time on Toto did.

Michel stood aside as excited passengers, like beads from a broken necklace, raced down the gangplank to discover Sainte Anne of Fair Island. He watched as men, women and children from the world over crowded about the town crier, who was to guide them into Sainte Anne.

Michel was as excited as they were. Had the Mayor remembered to send the announcement of the contest date?

As soon as the last passenger had stepped off the ship, a brown leather sack came sailing through the air and landed at the foot of the gangplank.

"Wake up, Michel Dupont," shouted a surly sailor. "It's your job to take the mail sack to the post office, you know. And here's a letter stamped with the Mayor's personal seal addressed to the artist Roger Lambert. You can take it along, too."

Michel reached for the important envelope. The seal was in the wrong place. It would be so easy to slip out the letter and read the news he had waited so long to hear.

But he turned away hurriedly from the ship and tempting thoughts, and in his haste, he bumped into one of the visitors—a strange man with a black beard and green eyes. Eyes that must see in the dark, thought Michel.

 54

"I have decided to stay," said the strange man haughtily. "Boy, take my valise to the inn!"

Michel felt uncomfortable, as if he had been squashed under the strange man's thumb. Could this be the visitor the birds had announced?

Holding the mail sack and the letter in one hand, Michel grabbed the valise impatiently with the other.

"Here, Michel, I'll help you," offered Charles Girard, who had lagged behind.

His pleasantness startled Michel. It was nice of Charles to take the suitcase now, but curious Charles didn't want the suitcase. He snatched the mail sack and the letter out of Michel's hand.

Michel started to protest, but he thought it wiser not to scrap over the mail in front of a visitor of Fair Island. So he grumbled something and started for the inn.

Quickly Charles Girard stuffed the letter into his pocket on a nest of soft feathers pulled from Josette's tail.

Only the gulls saw him. Only the gulls.

Softly Charles slipped away from the dock. Softly the tides slipped away, too. Away from the dock out to sea, hurrying in little runs and leaps, hurrying far, far from Charles Girard and the wickedness of his plans.

No one saw the stealthy boy come out of the post office and turn into the Pine Forest. Far from the music.

55

Far from the dancing into his hideaway castle, dark with towers of trees.

No one followed as Charles sat down on an old stump and opened the Mayor's letter to Roger Lambert.

The first page asked the artist to make posters for the contest, but where was the date? Had the Mayor forgotten again? Charles flipped over to the last page. Nothing. Nothing. His finger moved along the lines as he read. On

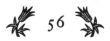

and on and on. Suddenly his eyes found the place. His finger jumped to that place. A postscript after the Mayor's signature, down at the bottom of the page.

July 19. Charles' upper lip curled disagreeably. That was the date of Michel's birthday. On July 19 Michel would be twelve, and any boy of twelve could participate in the contest!

Charles was afraid of Michel, afraid that Michel would win. How easy it would be to change the date of the contest! No one would ever know. A twist of the pen. A *19* into an *18*. July 18. And Michel would still be too young.

It would be so easy. The Mayor himself was such a forgetful man, and Charles knew the dark pines would never whisper his secret. The dark pines would never whisper his tale. If Michel did not compete, Charles would surely win.

July 18. An *8* was so close to a *9*. It would hardly be changing the date. Yet Michel had never hurt him. Perhaps, perhaps. Charles put the letter back into his pocket. For an instant, pine trees parted and opened their gates to the sun. Soft shafts of sun.

Charles shivered. He was cold. The sun did not warm him.

At his feet he found a flat stone, flat and smooth as the cover of a book. He used it as a desk. From his pocket he pulled out the letter again—and a pen.

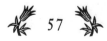

A *9* into an *8*. Charles practiced several times on a piece of scratch paper. Then, at the bottom of the Mayor's letter, from the straight stem of the *9*, he curved around to the right. Then upward to the left.

It wasn't too awkward a number; his nine turned into an eight. Charles Girard smiled. As he smiled, the pine trees closed their gates to the sun, and the winds of the changing tides grew cold.

Chapter 6

An Announcement

MICHEL waved to the men at their games as he raced across the green toward the square. How light he felt without that clumsy suitcase. Free from the stare of those catlike eyes. Comfortable again in the midst of gaiety and cheerful voices calling to him as he passed.

Had anyone noticed Roger Lambert or Charles Girard? Perhaps Maman would know! But Maman had been busy selling flowers, and she had not noticed.

"Holà, Michel, move. Move away from the table. You're hiding your mother's pretty flowers, and you will ruin my masterpiece."

Michel wondered where the voice was coming from. Finally he looked up into the old fig tree. Someone was up on his balcony branch. It was not Georges. Not Toto.

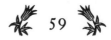 59

Black shoes, blue trousers, a white shirt and a red sash. Quickly Michel raced to see who had climbed where so few dared to go.

"Who is in my tree?" he called.

"Come up and see," answered a pleasant voice.

Michel recognized the pleasant voice. It was Roger Lambert, perched on the balcony branch.

"Have you seen Charles Girard? Did you get the Mayor's letter?" he asked, scrambling up into the high branches.

Roger Lambert looked surprised. "No one asked for me," he said. "In fact, I didn't think anyone knew I was here. It's the perfect sketching place," marveled the artist. "What is your fee for this wonderful tree?"

Michel felt proud, as proud as if Monsieur Lambert had stepped into Michel's own home to pay him a visit.

"It's not really my tree, Monsieur, but if I could see some of your sketches—"

"Wish granted," nodded Monsieur Lambert, handing over his pad. "Start from the back. I do things backward sometimes," he chuckled. "Just for the fun of it."

Michel rubbed his hands clean on the sides of his dark shorts. He propped himself up against the trunk of the tree and turned the pages.

The drawings were like pictures from a book. Perhaps someday they would be in a book about Sainte Anne. Michel turned the pages carefully. There was the Market

Square dressed up with banners and flags and festive decorations. There were costumes of southern France swirling with color. Soft shades, soft as the air of Provence. Bright tones, bright as the laughter of the people whom Roger Lambert liked to draw.

"They're wonderful, Monsieur. And I recognize everyone. There's Madame Mirabelle at her table of pies and cakes and apple tarts. And to her right—it's old Nanette working on a piece of lace. Madame Abélard is showing off her figs and dates. You haven't forgotten anyone."

Michel leaned over and pointed to the picture Roger Lambert was working on. "And who is that? Oh, now I know! It's Me Too's mother with her lovely coral beads. To the left is the Troubadour who recites the poetry of Provence. Oh! Here's Maman with her fragrant flowers making her way into your picture."

Roger worked swiftly, while Michel made pictures in his mind, pictures for The Lady with the Golden Voice. Soft shades, soft as the air of Provence. Bright tones, bright as the laughter of a gay and happy people.

Michel could see the artist had not finished. "Why did you leave this empty space here?" he asked curiously.

The artist's pencil darted into every corner of his page. "It's reserved for the children dancing the farandole. Go join them, Michel. I'd like you to be in it, too."

Michel wanted to find Charles Girard. But the excit-

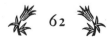

ing call of the flute and the tambourin, that long, long drum of Provence, drew him toward Georges and Toto and the children of Sainte Anne, as they danced on a carpet of sun. Twisting and turning, weaving and blending. Bright gay ribbons of color, dancing the farandole.

No one noticed when Charles finally came back into the village. A hush had fallen over the square. The orchestra was still. The clapping hands and dancing feet had stopped. No one spoke. No one buzzed excitedly over the coral necklace or the bits of lace.

Charles Girard trembled. Had everyone guessed his secret? Were they waiting to punish him now?

But Sainte Anne's visitors were not thinking about Charles Girard. They were listening to the soft voice of the Troubadour, who was filling their hearts with the poetry of Provence.

As he approached, Charles heard the soft poetry of Provence, but he was not moved by its beauty. He was eager to get rid of the Mayor's letter.

Quietly he crept up to Roger Lambert, who had come down from the old fig tree.

Quickly he showed him the Mayor's letter. "I'm sorry I didn't bring it sooner," he lied, "but I helped move some cargo on the *Silver Queen*."

"Let's see the letter," said Roger Lambert, believing the boy.

Charles smoothed out its wrinkles and handed it to the

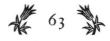

artist. "I shouldn't have put it in my pocket," he apologized.

Gently the Troubadour ended his farewell to the visitors of Sainte Anne. While the audience was still under its spell, Roger Lambert whispered to the town crier who, with a quick rat-tat-tat on his drum, asked for everyone's attention.

"I have some news which you have waited to hear for a long time, news which will please you, I'm sure. Our good Mayor has finally remembered to announce the date of the contest."

"The kind forgetful man," someone shouted.

The air echoed with cheers. Michel wiped his damp hot face with the back of his dusty hand, as the town crier continued.

"We know that all Sainte Anne will be here. We also hope that all of you visitors will be able to come back, too," the town crier continued, teasing his audience. "For on that day the Mayor and a board of judges will choose the Messenger of Fair Island. Messenger to The Lady with the Golden Voice."

"When? When? When?" shouted the crowd.

"Don't be so slow! We want to know!"

Michel was standing straighter than ever before, stretching into twelve years old as fast as he could.

For a moment Charles wished he could start his day all over again. But it was too late!

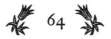 64

The town crier looked at the Mayor's letter as he spoke. "The date of the contest, ladies and gentlemen, is July eighteenth."

Michel bit his lip so hard that little spots of red smeared his front tooth.

What had happened? Why had the Mayor changed his mind?

Gone were Michel's hopes. Gone his dreams. Vanished The Lady with the Golden Voice. Vanished with the winds of the changing tides.

"Only eleven," sneered Charles Girard as he passed. "That's too bad!"

Chapter 7

Chariots of Rain

Only eleven, stormed Michel to the trees. Too young. That's all I'll ever be. Too young for anything.

The trees stirred in the wind, bending their heads as if to answer.

You're glad, stormed Michel at the moon. I can see it in your eyes—your mischievous eyes. You're glad.

But the moon, whose face was bright as gypsy fires, saw nothing—nothing but herself in the mirror of the sea.

"You're glad, too," the boy shouted to Georges and Toto, who were digging clams out on a sandbar.

When they heard his voice, they waved and laughed a friendly laugh.

Suddenly Michel threw down his basket and began to

dig into the bubbling sand. I'll be gay. I'll be gay like you, as he nodded toward the boys. I'll work. I'll work so hard that I'll forget my disappointment. Papa said I was brave. I'll show him that I'm brave and not too young.

Savagely he clawed at the air holes in the gold and silver sand. Savagely he dumped the wet cold clams into his basket—5-10-15-16-17-18-18. How he hated that number! July 18 was the day after tomorrow. How he hated the sound of an *18!*

He was still working when Georges and Toto stopped by to say good night.

Thirty-five—forty—forty-five—fifty.

At last Michel's basket was full. He picked it up and hurried away. Quickly away from the sea. Ghostly-looking was the market place when Michel passed. Here queer shapes were whispering secrets to each other. Here wispy shadows skipped about as the moon, tired of admiring herself in the sea, went strolling through the branches of the trees.

Suddenly the moon seemed to stop. Michel followed her glance. There on the wall was one of Roger Lambert's posters and that horrible date—July 18. Michel forgot the promise he had made himself. Into his basket flew his hand. 1-2-3-4-5-6. Six times, six clams dashed against the poster. Six smears of mud and sand.

In the darkness behind him, Michel did not hear the soft footsteps of the stranger with the black beard and the

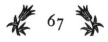

green eyes. Michel did not hear him glide away into the night.

Nor did he hear Roger Lambert until he spoke.

"I'm sorry you don't like my poster, Michel," said the artist gently. "Is the lettering poor? Or doesn't it have enough color?"

Michel was confused, confused by what he had done, and startled by Roger's kindness.

"I am sorry, Monsieur Lambert. Your posters are so beautiful. I guess—I guess I lost my temper.

"I was so sure the contest wouldn't take place before my twelfth birthday." Michel tried to brush away the spots on the poster as he kept talking. "I had so many things to tell The Lady with the Golden Voice."

Roger Lambert nodded understandingly. "When will you be twelve?"

"The nineteenth!" Michel coughed a little so Roger wouldn't hear the huskiness in his voice.

Strangely enough, the moon paled. Proud moon trying to escape the bank of clouds which held her prisoner.

The artist started to say something. He held out his hand as if to offer encouragement, but Michel darted away. Round the bend. Up the path. Up the hill to Half Way Point. And there in the stillness of night he listened to the nightingale.

"It's been practicing. Practicing for you," he murmured to The Lady with the Golden Voice.

68

At home Papa was all excited. "There's rain in the wind," he announced gaily.

Michel shrugged his shoulders. "The wind cannot always be trusted," he answered without smiling.

"Wait till you hear this," continued Papa cheerfully. "Pépère has rheumatism. And you know what that means—

> "'An old sailor in pain
> Brings tidings of rain.'"

This time Michel forgot his own disappointment and looked pleased. For he knew what a promise of rain meant to the people of Fair Island.

Suddenly Michel sputtered like a firecracker just before it explodes. "The rain!"

"Has it started?" asked Maman, quietly going to the window.

"No no no," shouted Michel. "I just realized what the rain might mean for me!"

During the night, while Michel tossed in his sleep, turtles left their homes and crawled to higher places. Rainbirds called to each other across the island. Poor Pépère felt stiff and sore, as he had not been for years.

"Rain," prayed Father Francis. "Please send rain. These farmers need it so badly!"

Over the ocean, storm clouds blackened the face of the moon and put out her orange fires. Roaring winds

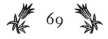

69

hurled mighty waves upon the rocky coast and watched them crumble into spray.

"Please," prayed Father Francis.

Over the rooftops of Sainte Anne came the clouds and from their depth the rain. Softly for a minute, so softly that no one heard. And then in long endless streams, pounding like the sea.

All the next morning Michel stood in front of the window and wished upon the raindrops. Hundreds of times he wished:

"Rain, oh, rain, please don't go away
Until I've had my twelfth birthday."

Papa and Maman watched the rain, too. "It will be over by nightfall, and the contest will be held tomorrow as announced," said Papa decidedly.

"I'm not so sure," answered Maman, who was sitting very close to the window. "I can hardly see to thread my needle. When it is that dark on Fair Island the rain usually lasts more than a day."

In black chariots of clouds it came, filling the cisterns, the wells, the thirsty gardens of Fair Island. Filling the hearts of the farmers with hope, the soul of Father Francis with thanks. "It's a good thing I fixed this roof last week," said Papa happily. "Now this house is as tight as the tin boxes upon your kitchen shelves, Maman."

"Oh, I'm glad you mentioned that!" exclaimed Maman, dropping her mending and hurrying out to the kitchen. "The rain has almost washed away my memory. Let me see," she mused. "Raisins? Yes. Spices? Plenty. Flour? I didn't know the flour box was so full. Now let me see," she hummed as she stretched to reach the sugar can.

Like a ballerina dancing, she balanced herself on her

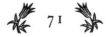 71

toes. Her hands reached up toward the shelf. She found the smooth sides of the box and her wrists stiffened to hold its weight. But up like a feather went the box. It felt like a child's block. Light and empty was the box.

Papa stood at the door, looking like a naughty puppy.

"It's all my fault," he said. "I bought flour at Monsieur Abélard's yesterday, and when Pépère came in to tell us about his rheumatism, I forgot all about the sugar. I'll go down and get some now."

Maman looked disappointed. "I did want to make Michel's birthday cake today, for if the weather clears, tomorrow will be Contest Day. We must be there even if Michel doesn't take part."

"I'll go down and get the sugar right away," Papa offered.

"But the wind and the rain. You will be blown away and washed right out to sea."

Papa laughed. "How right the Northerners are when they say we let our imaginations play tricks on us! You know I'll not be washed away to sea. There's no storm strong enough that can do that to me."

"The Northerners say we are great boasters, too," winked Maman.

"That's because we have so very much to boast about," exclaimed Michel, who had overheard. "Wait for me. I'm coming too. Maybe I can find out for sure about the contest."

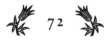

"I didn't know I had a Monsieur Me Too in the family," joked Papa. "Hurry! I'm ready to go."

On the way to the village they rescued Madame Scareaway. Madame Gypsy Scareaway, the only one besides Charles Girard who was not pleased with the rain.

"We can put her in the tool shed," said Papa. "Poor bundle of mud."

Michel untangled her earrings and pulled pebbles out of her hair.

"Don't you mind Papa," he soothed, propping her up. "Maman will wash your clothes, and then you'll be your own Scareaway self once more."

As Papa and Michel reached the village the rain stopped. Windows and doors banged open, and chattering voices replaced the drum, drum, drum of the rain.

Papa went to Monsieur Abélard's, while Michel crossed the square to talk to Toto, who was arguing with Charles Girard.

"It will clear up for tomorrow," laughed Charles in their faces. "The wind will dry up the roads, and we will have our contest. Too bad!"

Toto's eyes narrowed. As Charles walked away, out shot Toto's foot. Tripping, slipping, over went Charles into a sea of mud.

"Toto, you shouldn't have," exclaimed Michel, who tried to pull Charles out of the puddle.

But Charles didn't want to be helped. He sat there like a frog in a pond, his eyes bulging with anger.

Out of the corner of his bulging eye, he saw the Mayor, who had arrived early for the contest.

"He did it; Michel Dupont tripped me," he shouted.

Michel did not want the Mayor to know that Toto was to blame, so he said nothing.

Toto tried to explain that it was his own fault. But Charles' voice was so loud that the Mayor could hear no one else.

 74

Sadly he shook his head. "I have always heard such good reports about you, Michel Dupont. I'm sorry to think that you would do such a thing."

The Mayor, who loved making speeches, would have made one then and there, but the wind blew hard, and the rain started again.

"This settles it!" he exclaimed. "I hereby postpone the contest. It will not take place tomorrow."

Toto was so pleased for Michel that he hopped up and down like a jumping jack.

"You are splashing me, young man," said the Mayor sternly. But as he turned into Madame Mirabelle's shop, he smiled. These boys always reminded him of his own childhood days. When he was not so tall—and differently wise.

"Michel, Michel! The contest has been postponed. Aren't you glad?"

Michel was so excited he couldn't speak.

"Look, Michel, the posters are announcing it, too."

July 18 had blurred. Streams of black paint were pouring down the paper and the eight was turning into a nine—the way it should have been all along.

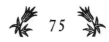

Chapter 8

On Your Mark

A THOUSAND mirrors of dew sparkled on their frames of grass at Half Way Point.

Look at yourself, Michel, they seemed to say. Look at your laughing eyes and happy smile, and never, never change.

Michel was waiting for Toto at Half Way Point. I'm twelve, he thought over and over again. I'm twelve. And today is the day of the contest!

Across a sea of sweet lavender and tender grass, Frisk was chasing something.

A jolly, frolicking puppy with a short wagging tail, a turned-up nose, and flippy-floppy ears chasing a butterfly. When he saw Michel, he came running to him.

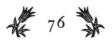

76

"Where's your master, Monsieur Frisk. He didn't forget, did he?"

A clear, bright whistle dancing with excitement answered his question. Round and round went the tune like bicycle wheels cutting corners—coasting down a hill, down Christopher Hill in the morning.

"Hello, Michel. I've got good news for you," shouted Toto, giving his bicycle bell an important ring. "The other day after you left, I saw the Mayor at Monsieur Abélard's."

"You didn't trip him, I hope," laughed Michel.

"I told him I was the one who pushed Charles Girard in the mud. I told him you had nothing to do with it."

"What did he say?" asked Michel anxiously.

"He said I was a brave boy to storm a mighty fortress and confess. But never to do it again. So you see, Michel, he doesn't blame you any more."

Michel pumped Toto's hand. "Such a good friend!" he said over and over.

As Toto gave Michel his bicycle, he gave it a proud pat. "I've oiled and polished it and tested it on Christopher Hill," he said. "Now it should fly like an arrow on the wings of the wind." Down below, the crowd swirled with impatience, and bright banners snapped their fingers with the breeze. "You'd better go, Michel. The contest will be starting soon."

Michel pushed Toto's bicycle toward the white start-

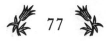

77

ing string stretched across the square. He was glad to have a handlebar to hold on to, for his knees felt shaky and his heart was beating faster than it ever had before.

Suddenly the watching crowd began to laugh. The Mayor, who was staring at his enormous gold watch, looked up, adjusted his glasses and began to laugh, too.

Michel wondered what could be so funny on such a solemn day. His eyes traveled down the line of waiting boys. Eleven of them, strong and straight and standing stiffly, waiting for the starting gun to send them spinning off into the hills. There were Georges and Jacques and Pierre and Charles Girard and all the rest. Each one promising himself that this race would be the beginning of his trip to The Lady with the Golden Voice.

Then Michel saw why the crowd was so amused. At the end of the line, small as a toothpick in a grove of trees, was little four-year-old. With his three-wheeler he had come to join the older boys.

"I'm going, too," he said proudly to Michel.

"Go home, pest," snarled Charles. "You're holding up the race."

The others spoke more kindly. But Me Too refused to move.

"Here comes the Mayor. He's going to put you in jail," yelled Charles.

Michel took Me Too's hand. "Monsieur Le Maire," he said politely, "don't you have a job for this little boy?"

"Of course, of course," nodded the Mayor, who had
no idea what sort of job he could pull out of his imagina-
tion.

"Let me see," he paused. "Why!" He cleared his
throat. "I have it!" But the Mayor hadn't thought of
anything.

Michel came to his rescue. "Did you say starter, Monsieur Le Maire?"

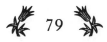 79

"Of course, of course, my very words," sputtered the Mayor, who loved children but never knew what to say to them. "But isn't he too little to shoot the starting gun?" The Mayor polished the face of his watch with a big red handkerchief.

"Monsieur Le Maire, Pépère is supposed to shoot the starting gun. But when the starting gun goes off, couldn't Me Too just cut the string which is holding us back?"

"Of course, of course. My very thought," said the Mayor with a smile, who always liked happy endings to his problems. "Come, my child, you may stand beside me and I will lend you my knife."

At first Monsieur Me Too wasn't sure that he wanted to stand beside the Mayor, but when he saw the Mayor's knife, he laughed. Monsieur Me Too liked shiny things. And the Mayor was handing him this shiny thing for him to use on the white starting string stretched across the square.

Snapping banners curled and uncurled their bright colors in the breeze. Rows of people cheered their good, kind Mayor. A few fond parents, like loose strands of wool in an unfinished tapestry, slipped out of the crowd to wish their sons good luck.

Michel waved to Papa and Maman just before they blurred into a mass of curious onlookers.

Then he turned to watch the judges' stand and saw the Mayor shake hands with Roger Lambert. Two colored

pencils and a pad were sticking out of the artist's shirt pocket. Monsieur Abélard was there too, and Monsieur Gabriel, the innkeeper.

Pépère was standing on the side lines holding the starting gun high in the air.

"Holà, Pépère. Be sure not to shoot holes in the bicycle tires," someone shouted.

"Maybe he's getting tired of fish for dinner and wants pigeons instead," someone else answered.

Pépère laughed and the crowd started to sing: "Là monteras-tu la côte, Pierrot? Là monteras-tu la côte? Can you climb that hill, Pierrot? Can you climb that hill?"

Michel straddled his bike and adjusted the pedals.

"I'm down here today. Not on the balcony watching," he told himself excitedly.

It was time. Un, deux, trois—one, two, three. The Mayor waved his red handkerchief.

Pépère wrinkled his nose and pulled the trigger. Me Too sawed at the starting string with the Mayor's shiny knife.

Nothing happened.

"Give it a whack," whispered the Mayor.

WHACK! The string fell to the ground as if it had been a slender spiderweb. The boys were off, all twelve of them, off to conquer a dark-gray giant cooling its head in the clouds.

At first the road was a golden twist of ribbon sprinkled

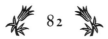

with tiny white pebbles and patches of fine powdered sand.

Over its rumpled surface sped the boys, crunching along, spitting sprays of sand through the spokes of their wheels.

Michel slowed down a little. He was going too fast on such a twisty road. In curves it ran, fringing a basin of blue. Then upward, upward it rose, narrowing like a sword's point cutting its way into the sky.

Michel wondered if they would all make it. Georges was already off, puffing like a steam engine.

"All right, Georges?" he asked.

Georges nodded a couple times. He couldn't waste his breath on words.

In the middle of the road Michel found a smooth strip, the width of his tire. There he stayed, pumping his bicycle ever nearer to the top of Christopher Hill.

"There goes Georges," shouted one of the boys.

Michel turned around. Georges had pulled to the side of the winding trail. Michel stopped.

A minute out of my time won't matter much, thought Michel. Just so I make the trip in two hours. "You're not hurt, are you, Georges?"

"Go on, Michel," protested Georges, gasping for breath. "It's my left knee. It feels as stiff as if I had been swimming in the English Channel. I'm almost as wet, too," he added.

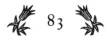

83

"Try rubbing it, Georges. That may take the pain away."

Georges looked grateful, but Michel could tell that he had given up. So had two other boys farther down the road.

When Michel hopped back on his bike again, a nasty little breeze jumped out from a forest of evergreens and twirled itself around him.

If it would only get behind me and push, wished Michel. But the breeze stayed in front—a barricade of cold air holding him back.

Michel tried to slice his way through the layers of wind, pedaling harder than he had ever pedaled before, and wondering all the time why he had forgotten to borrow Papa's watch.

At the top of the hill Monsieur Domino was waiting to check the boys' names as they came by.

Michel could see him in a clearing. He didn't look much like a teacher today as he paced back and forth like a soldier on sentry duty.

I won't ever be able to say "bonjour," my throat is aching so! he thought.

Stinging little waves of dizziness tempted him to turn— to drift into the cool green shade of cypress trees. To splash his hands and feet in the frosty streams that bubbled by.

But Michel kept on. On and on. Until the "soldier"

 84

pacing back and forth looked more and more like his teacher marching up and down the room at examination time.

Monsieur Domino did not expect Michel to say "bonjour."

"Rest yourself, lad," he said kindly. "And have some peppermints. I bought them at Monsieur Abélard's this morning. They'll cool your thirsty throat."

Michel pointed to Monsieur Domino's watch.

"The time? You have broken a record for coming up Christopher Hill. You made it in an hour."

Michel slid off his bike, Toto's bike, and threw himself into a patch of soft grass. Into the softness of grass he sprawled while sleep came by and almost tucked him in.

Suddenly a spray of sand stinging the side of his face made him jump quickly to his feet. It was Charles Girard scrunching by, over the top of the hill and swiftly down.

"Hurry, Michel! You'd better be on your way. The road down is just as narrow and has more curves than the road coming up." Now Monsieur Domino was the classroom teacher giving advice.

"Merci, merci," called Michel, testing the brakes on Toto's bicycle. "This is going to be fun. No hands! Here I go!"

Monsieur Domino adjusted his pocket telescope. Two boys were crawling toward him, like turtles still in the race. "They may make it in time," he said softly.

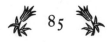 85

Training his telescope on the other side of the hill, he watched Michel twisting down the road, as graceful as a skier on snow-covered trails. A few turns below, Charles had stopped his bicycle. A flat tire? wondered Monsieur Domino. He adjusted his telescope again. Charles was tugging at something, something big and brown and heavy-looking.

Monsieur Domino's hand trembled. It couldn't be. And yet, stretched across the road with no passing space, a terrible trap lay blocking the road, waiting for Michel to come by.

86

"Michel! Michel!" screamed Monsieur Domino in a voice which Michel would not have recognized, if he had heard it. "Look out below. Look out! There's a log —a big log."

Law law law law, echoed the forest drearily, in muffled tones.

La la la la la, sang the wind. And Michel sang with it, as it cooled his face and tickled his eyes.

It won't be long now, he thought. Soon I shall be sailing into Sainte Anne faster than an arrow from an archer's bow.

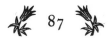

Michel had said "no hands" at the top of Christopher Hill. But that was awhile ago. There were too many dangerous twists in the road for "no hands" now. And with each turn Michel seemed to gain speed.

I hope this road doesn't come to a dead end, thought Michel. And just as he imagined a sudden ending to his wild race, he saw the log.

Michel's first thought was for Toto's bike. It would be smashed to pieces against this lifeless hulk of wood. He tried the brakes. It was too late. The thick brown bark was already reaching out for the front wheel. With all his strength Michel pulled upward on the handlebars. The front tire skimmed over the log. Up came the back of the bike. Higher, higher. Michel had seen a man jump his motorcycle over a barrel once. Now he was jumping, too. Over, over, over went the back wheel, whirring scornfully at the lifeless log.

Michel had avoided the trap. But now he couldn't control his bike. It swerved to one side, to the other, as if it were trying to dodge a pursuing swarm of bees.

Michel stood on the brakes. The bicycle came to a sudden, undamaged stop, and Michel went sailing head-first over the handlebars.

Chapter 9

Discovery and Disappointment

T HE path which Michel had been following stretched before him like a narrow landing strip built upon a mountain ledge.

To his right, gray cliff, sliced clean for half a mile, plunged steeply to the valley below. To his left, small pine trees bristled like the quills of a porcupine on guard.

At the top of Saint Christopher Hill, Monsieur Domino's hands were shaking with such excitement when he saw Michel clear the log that he dropped his telescope.

"I would never have believed it," he exclaimed. "He made it! He cleared the log. A daredevil acrobat, ce Michel."

Monsieur Domino breathed a sigh of relief and sat down on the campstool he had brought with him. That

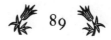

young man will reach the village before Charles Girard, he thought.

But the dropped telescope had not seen Michel turning head over heels in the air.

Head over heels went Michel. Over and over to the edge of the road and down. Down a pine-covered slope he rolled, just missing the quills of trees and the spearing branches.

Michel was so stunned by his fall that he lay on a carpet of dry pine needles, unable to see the bearded face and the green eyes that peered down at him.

"One of the racers. He'll be out for a while," muttered the dark stranger. "I'll have time to finish what I'm doing before he comes to."

Quickly he returned to the clearing where he had packed something in a large box filled with straw. Several small objects were lying on the ground next to him. One by one he picked them up. Then with careful fingers he wrapped them in paper and buried them in the mysterious box. So absorbed in his work had he become that he did not notice Michel. Michel stirred. Then he sat up. Sharp red and blue streaks of light jabbed at his eyes, and trees were spinning like horses on a merry-go-round.

Michel doubled his fists and stared at his wrists. "That will keep you from getting dizzy," Papa had told him once.

At first it wouldn't work. His fists jumped toward him

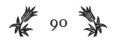

as if they were going to punch him in the nose. But Michel kept staring. Staring and looking up until the dizzy, whirly feeling left him, until fuzzy shapes turned into green trees again, and the black smudge in the clearing became a man bending over a mysterious box.

Suddenly Michel remembered that he must hurry down to the village, down to the Mayor with his speech to The Lady with the Golden Voice. His fingers tingled. Minutes were passing through them so quickly he could not hold them back.

"Monsieur, Monsieur," he called. "Quelle heure est-il? Have you a watch? How long have I been lying here?"

The mysterious stranger jumped as Michel approached.

"Have I been here long?" repeated Michel.

"How should I know?" snapped the man. "Get out of here and mind your own business."

"I won't bother you," smiled Michel. "Don't you remember me? I carried your suitcase to the hotel when you got off the *Silver Queen*." With each word Michel advanced a step, getting closer and closer to the five puppetlike figures propped on the ground beside the brown box.

The five little figures looked straight ahead, silent little statues unmoved by Michel's excited curiosity and the stranger's anger.

Suddenly the man's voice softened. "Would you like to see my treasures?" he asked politely. "You won't believe it. But they're Roman statues, two thousand years old!"

Now the man was smiling. "I've been digging for days," he added. "It was to be a surprise. But never mind, go tell the Mayor and the others, and I shall stay here on guard."

Michel could hardly speak! Roman ruins on Fair Island! Statues, bowls, perhaps a theater buried under Christopher Hill. All of France would hear of this. The news would spread throughout Europe, to America, all over the world. If he hurried, he might still have time to recite to the Mayor the message he had kept in his heart

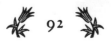 92

for The Lady with the Golden Voice, bursting forth at the end with the news of this marvelous discovery.

Michel bent over to tie his shoelace. I've done enough falling for one day. This is not the time to trip. As he made a special double knot, his eyes blurred and his head began to swim.

"Ho-ho, young man!" The soft smiling voice disappeared. "Do you really think I want the Mayor to know about these Roman ruins? Not when they've been waiting here two thousand years for me to discover," he said with a sneer.

"This is my treasure, and I shall share it with no one, not when it means a fortune for me!"

Quickly he packed the statues into the box. Loudly he snapped the lid, as he turned toward Michel.

"Good-by, young man," he said. "Would you like to know my plans? First I shall bring your bicycle back here, so that the game will not be too easy for those who come to look for you. Then I shall join my servant, who will be waiting in the cove to take me back to the Mainland, and you will never be troubled by the bearded stranger again."

But Michel did not hear. He did not see. Michel had fainted again.

At the top of Christopher Hill, Monsieur Domino trained his telescope on the two boys who were still in the race.

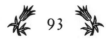 93

Slowly like the tortoise in the story, they arrived. Slow but sure. Jacques Vernier and Pierre Martel.

Monsieur Domino told them of the log in the path. "It was about two miles from here that Michel made his exciting jump." He pointed. "On that straight piece of road that looks like a string from here."

"See?" He passed his telescope to Jacques.

Jacques stood on tiptoe. "Why, the log is still in the path!" he exclaimed. "Michel forgot to move it away."

Monsieur Domino was puzzled. "That's strange. It doesn't sound like Michel. He knew that we would be coming down the hill, too."

Pierre was getting restless. "We haven't much time. Let's get started."

"Don't forget to slow down for the log," shouted Monsieur Domino.

"Make way for our magic wheels," laughed Pierre.

"Look out below," shouted Jacques. And away they flew into the whistling wind.

Monsieur Domino came more slowly. His bicycle, Undependable, was not always to be trusted on these steep hills. So, like an ant circling the inside of an unfamiliar sugar bowl, he came. Very slowly until he reached the log which the boys had pulled to the side of the road. As he sent it spinning into the gorge half a mile below, he wondered what he should do.

The Mayor must be told about Charles Girard. Yet

94

Monsieur Domino was anxious about Michel. It seemed so strange that he had not moved the log. Perhaps, perhaps something had happened. Perhaps like the log, Michel and the bike had disappeared into the torrent below.

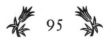 95

Deep worry frowns wrinkled Monsieur Domino's forehead. "Charles Girard can wait," he said out loud. "I'm afraid something has happened to Michel! Holà, Michel! Où es-tu? Where are you?" His voice fell into the torrent. His voice touched the tall trees. "Michel! Michel!"

Monsieur Domino searched the forest, calling until his throat was dry and his words echoed like rustling leaves.

If only the birds could speak, he thought. They would tell me where to look.

Just as he was ready to give up, he heard a faint cry.

"Monsieur Domino, here I am! Here I am, Monsieur!"

The deep worry frowns rippled away, as Monsieur Domino hurried to the sound of Michel's voice. At least the boy was alive.

Michel was too excited to answer Monsieur Domino's questions.

"Roman ruins!" he kept repeating. "Roman ruins, Monsieur, we must go see if there are more."

Monsieur Domino smiled pleasantly. "You'll be all right, Michel. The ruins will disappear when you feel better."

"But it's true, Monsieur. He was packing statues in a wooden box. Roman figures, two thousand years old!"

Monsieur Domino wondered if Michel had been struck on the head. Blows of this kind sometimes make people see strange things that do not exist, he thought.

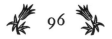

"We can talk about Roman ruins later, Michel. Now, if you feel well enough, we must continue down to the village," he urged. "There are many things I must explain to the Mayor and to the people of Sainte Anne. If you are strong enough, try it, Michel. I know they will want to hear your speech to The Lady with the Golden Voice."

"But it's too late, Monsieur," answered Michel sadly. "Charles Girard is now Messenger of Fair Island, I'm sure."

"Not if I can help it," muttered Monsieur Domino. "Let's go, Undependable. You'll have to be on your best behavior on the way down, for I'm not going to put on the brakes this trip."

Down the hill they raced, like snowballs picking up speed as they rolled.

Undependable behaved very well. She did not even try to show off before the crowds, as her rider guided her right up to the Mayor's stand.

Toto's bike wanted to follow Undependable. But Michel brought it to a stop behind the crowd, hoping no one would see him.

With one ear he listened to Charles Girard. With the other he listened to himself. Be a good sport. Be a good sport, he repeated. Don't let them see you care.

Charles was making a fine speech, and everyone seemed surprised.

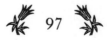

"Pas mal," they said. "Not bad." "Very good!" "Excellent!"

The applause was long and loud.

Michel turned toward Half Way Point. There he would take his dream from his heart and look at it once more. There he would open wide his hands and watch his dream float away on the crest of sweet lavender and tender grass.

Chapter 10

Messenger of
Fair Island

Michel! Michel! Where have you been?"
Toto tried to stop his friend. "What in the world happened to you? What are those marks on your face? And
those tears in your clothes?"

Toto's questions held on to each other like freight cars
on a speeding train.

"Millions of things happened, Toto. But I'll tell you
about them later," Michel whispered, as he kept moving
away from the crowd.

"Don't go away now, Michel," Toto tried again. "The
Mayor has a very important announcement to make.
You've got to come back."

Frisk, too, wanted Michel to stay. So he ran around
him in big circles, barking as fast as Toto had talked.

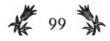

99

Michel grinned. "All right, Frisk. You win. After all, I guess I should stay to congratulate Charles."

Frisk kept on barking, even after the boys had mixed in with the crowd.

Finally the Mayor frowned and stopped talking.

"Sh," said Toto. "Listen."

There was a dramatic minute of silence. The crowd braced itself. The air stiffened.

"What I have to tell you now," continued the Mayor, "saddens me very much. I have just learned that a member of our community has disgraced himself. Today, in order to win honor and praise, he almost brought about great harm to one of our contestants. I was pleased with this young man. I had high hopes for him. Alas, I was wrong. This boy has failed. Failed because he cheated to gain success. Charles Girard, come here."

The crowd said nothing. In a path of silence Charles came to the Mayor's stand.

"Charles Girard, you have just made a speech. Now I want you to make another one. Tell the crowd what Monsieur Domino told me. When you've finished that, tell them what you did to the letter I sent to Fair Island. Roger Lambert showed my letter to a handwriting expert, who says that the date of the contest was changed. Explain this to our friends who cheered you and trusted you a few minutes ago."

Gray with fear, his voice shaking with sobs, Charles told about the letter and the log.

"You might have killed Michel," shouted Pépère. The crowd groaned, and bright banners overhead snapped scornfully in the wind.

After a while Father Francis, who had been talking to the Mayor, raised his hands and asked the crowd to listen. He too had something to say.

"Fair Island is a lovely island," he said softly. "Fair in beauty and fair in spirit. Charles Girard, in any other town you would be sent away to a special school. But you are young, and one of ours. So the Mayor and I are going to give you another chance. You will be allowed to stay on Fair Island, at the rectory with me."

"He should be punished," the people shouted angrily.

Monsieur Me Too thought they were talking about him.

"No no no, I've been a good boy!" he exclaimed.

No one laughed this time. There was too much anger in the crowd. Finally, the other contestants were called.

"Jacques Vernier, Pierre Martel and Michel Dupont.

"Where is Michel?"

The three boys came up to the platform and faced the judges' stand.

Jacques and Pierre talked about five minutes. But they were very tired, and their speeches sounded tired, too.

"Thank you," said the Mayor kindly. "Climbing Christopher Hill is indeed a difficult job. Now, Michel, my boy, before you recite your invitation to The Lady with the Golden Voice, tell us what happened."

Bright and vivid were Michel's words, as they went flying over the handlebars of Toto's bike. Quick and colorful were his words as they invited the crowd to go sailing with him through the trees and down the steep banks into the clearing.

Suddenly the words stopped. Michel turned toward the Mayor. "Please, may I save the most exciting part for the last?" he begged.

"Like dessert," shouted Monsieur Me Too.

The Mayor smiled and nodded, and Michel started his speech to The Lady with the Golden Voice.

He spoke with politeness and praise. He filled his speech with bright pictures and poetry, with love of Fair Island and with admiration for The Lady with the Golden Voice.

The Mayor took out his red handkerchief and blew his nose. The judges looked at one another in surprise, while those in the audience whispered to one another that they had never seen Fair Island in such a lovely light before.

Michel's eyes danced with excitement. "This is what I shall include in my speech to The Lady with the Golden Voice," he said, and he bowed and smiled mysteriously.

"Somewhere on Christopher Hill you will find—you will find Roman ruins, coins, bowls, statues, a theater perhaps, waiting proudly to show themselves to you, The Lady with the Golden Voice."

The Mayor almost fell off his chair. "Michel, what are you saying? I'm afraid you were hurt more seriously than we realized. Sit down, my boy."

But Michel did not want to sit down.

"Monsieur Domino thought it was a blow on my head," he laughed. "But look, I have no bump. I'm very sure I'm right."

The Mayor nodded again. So then and there Michel told his listeners about the man with the black beard and the green eyes.

"Horrible!" groaned the crowd.

"Let me take you to the spot," pleaded Michel. "Please."

The Mayor did not know what to do. This was perhaps the most exciting thing that ever happened to Fair Island. Michel was so positive. On the other hand, perhaps the boy had imagined it all.

"Allons-y! Let's go," shouted the crowd. "To the buried treasure," they sang.

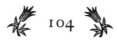 104

The Mayor waved his red handkerchief toward Saint Christopher Hill. "All right, Michel."

Someone found a hoe. Someone else a pitchfork and a spade. All together, as if under a spell, they followed Michel up the bicycle trail of Christopher Hill.

Georges, Toto and Frisk caught up with Michel. So did Papa and Maman after a while.

"We're proud of you, son," they said. And that was all they were able to say, for Michel was going so fast they had to save their breath for the rest of the climb.

Monsieur Domino pointed out a smear in the road. "This is where Charles Girard left the log," he said.

The crowd gasped as they looked into the torrent a half a mile below. Maman's hand trembled when she took Michel's and held it very tightly.

Suddenly Michel turned toward his friends. "We're almost there," he said. "Down this slope to the clearing, then through an archway of trees."

"Do we have to sail through the air the way you did?" someone called out.

Michel grinned and hurried on, while the crowd followed down the narrow slope, like a laughing brook swirling with sunshine. Here and there the laughing brook bubbled over, as children slipped out of the line and raced ahead.

When at last they had reached the clearing, the Mayor asked everyone to stop.

"We hope to discover the ruins Michel talked about," he said. "But don't be too disappointed if the mysterious stranger removed the entire treasure."

If there was a treasure, thought Monsieur Domino.

"Then too," continued the Mayor, "tread lightly. Walk with care. Pretend you are entering a fragile glass case. And be ready to stop immediately if we ask you to do so."

"Ho, Michel! What shall I do with my excitement?" yelled Toto.

"Put it in your pocket," answered Monsieur Me Too from his perch on his father's shoulder.

"Bravo, Monsieur Me Too," exclaimed the Mayor. "From now on, you will have to help me write my speeches. Yes, keep your excitement in your pockets, until it is time to take it out and celebrate."

The Mayor was still talking, but Michel could wait no longer. Through the avenue of trees he went, stooping to examine every mushroom, every shiny leaf. But he found nothing. No coins, no bowls, no statues.

Had Monsieur Domino been right? Had it been a dream?

Suddenly something ran past him. It was Frisk, who had no pocket in which to put his excitement.

"Stop him!" shouted the Mayor. "He may do some damage."

Michel knew there was nothing to harm, but he ran

after Frisk. Zigzagging through the woods he dashed, trying to stop the puppy with the flippy-floppy ears and the short wagging tail.

Frisk paid no attention to Michel's calls. Quickly he scurried through an opening in an old stone wall. The opening was too small for Michel. So he boosted himself to the top of the wall and jumped down on the other side onto a bed of leaves. A big jump, a strong jump which ended in a gasp of surprise.

Michel couldn't stop. There was no earth under the bed of leaves, no earth under his feet.

The leaves crackled against his ankles. They scratched the sides of his legs. They stuck to his shirt. They tickled his ears and filled his eyes with dust.

Michel couldn't stop. Michel was going through the bed of leaves—down, down into a hole, down like a dart piercing dark emptiness.

An old abandoned well, he thought. If I could only just grab some of that ivy. It would break my fall!

A tangle of vine grew helpfully near Michel's outstretched hand. He tried to catch hold of it. Once, twice, three times it slipped through his fingers.

Once more Michel grabbed. This time he caught the old gnarled rope of vine and held on. The palm of his hand felt as if it were being burned by a flame. Still Michel held on, twisting, jerking, sliding swiftly till he reached the bottom of the dried old well.

How good to be on solid ground again, instead of swinging back and forth like the clapper on a bell!

He braced himself firmly against a wall and looked up. Far above, a sparkle of sun winked at him. Hurry back, it seemed to say.

Hurrying back up this deep shaft of shadows won't be so easy, thought Michel, tearing off the sleeve of his shirt to make a bandage. If I could only find another way out. This sore hand may give me trouble.

Michel sat down to bandage his hand, and as he propped himself against the wall, he felt the earth loosen behind him. What sort of well was this?

Suddenly his heart began to beat wildly. Could this be the spot he had been looking for? Could this be an entrance to more buried treasure?

His excitement made him forget the hurt in his hand. Pulling off one of his sandals, he used it to scoop away the dirt.

On and on he worked, forgetting the time, forgetting the crowd above.

Then suddenly his arm shot through another hole. Michel did not hesitate. Quickly he made it large enough to crawl into.

Into thick darkness he started. Into the low winding passageway on hands and knees he crawled. Then unexpectedly his hand failed to find the sandy floor.

Michel snapped back and sat on his heels. Ahead of

him the path had dropped, dropped into emptiness and more darkness. Michel felt as if a trap door had opened in front of him.

"I'll toss these pebbles down," he said out loud.

His voice sounded warm in the dampness around him.

The pebbles did not drop very far. So Michel turned around slowly and grasped the ledge at the end of the tunnel. Slowly he lowered himself into nothingness until the toes of his sandals scratched against a rough sand floor.

Michel heard a hum of voices. Were the ancient spirits coming forward to protect their treasure?

Oooooooo! Michel took one step forward. Then another and another. Something made him stop, something he had almost stepped on. His hand stirred the air around it. Then cautiously he stroked the invisible object; it didn't jump, and it didn't bite. As he grabbed it, it fell in all directions. Parts to the right, parts to the left, some went scurrying across the floor. Michel picked up one of the pieces. It was round and hard; so was the next piece and the next.

"I think I've crumbled a mountain of Roman coins," he gasped. "A mountain of coins that has not been disturbed for over a thousand years."

Michel was sure the mysterious stranger with the black beard had never entered this cave; those treasures came from another spot. This was Michel's own discovery.

Michel picked up one of the coins. He would show the people that it was not a blow on the head that made him speak of Roman treasures. As he pushed the coin deep into his pocket, his fingernail nicked something he had forgotten about—a match, an old, old match. He rubbed it against his sandal. Nothing happened. He tried again and again, until at last there was a sputter—a dancing flame, a tiny blaze of light in the darkness.

"Michel! Michel!" The spirits were calling him by name, now that they could see his face.

Michel shivered. Then he laughed out loud.

These were not spirits; they were Papa and Maman and the Mayor and his friends looking for him.

How he must hurry! How he must go to them and tell them what he had seen—the bowls, the jars, the statues—when the flame danced lightly on its tiny stick.

Michel went back the way he came. This time he could hardly wait to face the crowd, to show what he had found. Slowly toward the light he crawled.

As he reached the hole into which he had tumbled, Papa was letting down a ladder made of men's sweaters.

"Climb aboard, Messenger of Fair Island," yelled the Mayor. "We'll give you a ride."

Michel was so excited he could hardly get on. "Messenger of Fair Island," the Mayor had called him.

Michel held on with one hand. In the other he carried his Roman coin, with designs two thousand years old.

110

"Handle with care," he warned.

The people roared with pleasure as Michel showed them what he had found.

"The man on the Roman coin seems happy to have been brought out of hiding. Why, he's almost smiling," said the Mayor.

"He can't be happier than I am," laughed Michel, who suddenly remembered that besides being Messenger of Fair Island, he still had a delicious birthday cake waiting for him at home!

111

Chapter 11

The Lady with the Golden Voice

THE birthday cake disappeared quickly. The days flew by as Michel practiced his speech. Finally, one morning, the town crier made the announcement that they had waited so long to hear. The Lady with the Golden Voice had not forgotten her promise.

"Tonight, if the weather is clear, she will sail from the Mainland and anchor her ship close to Fair Island."

Michel wished for a moment that he had not come down to the edge of the water alone.

I must stay calm, he thought, as he stood on the raft which was to take him out on the sea. I must be calm, or I shall never be able to make my speech to The Lady with the Golden Voice.

He examined the paddle Pépère had given him, smooth and strong and comfortable to hold. He dipped it into the sea, into the lavender lanes of sea made by the setting sun.

It won't be long, he thought, and as he thought, he began to look for the stars and wish for the moon.

Slowly all his friends came down from the village, too. On ledges of rock they sat. High in the hills and close to the shore, speaking in low tones, afraid to disturb the moon.

Then down the path, down the sandy path came the Mayor and Monsieur Domino bringing the children of Sainte Anne. Each child carried confetti, and each had a candle in his hand.

"You know where to stand," said Monsieur Domino. "We have practiced it many times before. Yes, yes, that's right."

"Do we light the candles now?" asked Monsieur Me Too, feeling as important as the Messenger of Fair Island.

"No, no, not yet. You must wait," repeated Monsieur Domino patiently.

The children said, "Oui, Monsieur!" They liked Monsieur Domino.

Suddenly everyone exclaimed, "Oh! La lune! The moon!"

It was the same orange moon Michel remembered so well. But tonight she had not come to tease Michel with

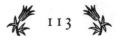

her gypsy fires nor to admire herself in the sea. Tonight she had come to guide The Lady with the Golden Voice toward the people of Fair Island.

Michel, who was getting restless, walked among his friends. "Good luck! Good luck!" they said.

Then a disappointed silence fell over the crowd. The moon had come as a pilot light, but still no boat appeared.

Suddenly someone called, "I see something—there, there on the right!"

It was nothing but the old fort at the bend of the cape. The old fort with window slits like eyes, waiting and watching, too.

The children stretched and began to hum. "Maybe she is lost, and our singing will lead her here," they said.

Perhaps the children were right. Perhaps she heard the humming of their tunes. Suddenly beneath a ceiling of stars appeared a beautiful boat floating toward Fair Island.

Excitement ran through the crowd. Swiftly it ran from those who sat on the high cliff to Michel and the children on the crescent shore.

"Shall we light the candles now?" asked the children, chirping like small birds on a branch.

"No, no, not yet." Monsieur Domino shook his head.

Slowly the boat advanced down the silvery strip of sea, like a dream from a world of magic make-believe. Closer, much closer than anyone had expected.

The crowd applauded as they had never applauded before. Michel dropped his paddle and the children forgot to light their candles. It was not until The Lady had finished her first song that they remembered to spell out *Welcome* with their tiny flickers of light.

Michel wondered when he should start. If he interrupted her singing, she might be displeased. If he waited too long, the boat could turn and disappear into the night, as it had done before.

I will wait a little longer, he thought, listening with all his heart to the tears and laughter of simple folk tunes, to the pageantry and splendor of the past.

There were songs for everyone on Fair Island. Gay dancing tunes, lively marching tunes, and lullabies filled with the love and tenderness of France.

Now, now it's time, the moon and the tides seemed to whisper. Now, echoed the people of Fair Island.

Yes, now, strummed the lute of The Lady with the Golden Voice.

Pépère gave the raft a push. Michel gripped his paddle, dipping it into the tides that led the way—straight toward the ship anchored in silver strands of sea.

After a while Michel's arms relaxed. His strokes grew steady and sure.

Suddenly he gasped. He could see more clearly now this floating stage for The Lady with the Golden Voice. He could see more clearly now the beautiful person

standing on a tiny balcony overlooking a garden of flowers and blossoming orange trees.

She will never want to leave this lovely stage and come
to us, thought Michel, as The Lady with the Golden
Voice signaled to her crew.

Slowly the ship moved. Softly the lute played music
for its voyage.

Michel closed his eyes. He could not watch The Lady's departure.

But the ship was not returning to the Mainland. It was
coming to meet Michel, coming so close that it touched
his raft and made him open his eyes.

The Lady had turned away from the edge of her balcony. Like a beautiful princess dressed for a ball, she
came down the stairs, majestically, in a thousand twinkling lights reflected by the sea. Her smile was warm as
she looked at Michel, her eyes like the songs she sang.

At a nod of her head, a gesture of her hand, Michel
stepped into the garden of flowers.

"I am Michel, Messenger of Fair Island," he said,
bowing. "I have a special favor to ask of you."

The Lady with the Golden Voice seemed surprised.
"A message for me?"

She hesitated a moment. Then she spoke to her crew.
"Pole our ship closer to the sandy shore," she said. "Per-
haps the people of Fair Island would like to hear their
Messenger. I know he speaks for them, too."

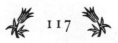

117

The crowd rose and cheered as the ship touched the rim of the island.

The Lady had returned to her balcony, and Michel, in the garden of flowers, looked up at her.

"O Fair and Lovely Lady!" he began. "Once upon a time you came to us and won our hearts with your beautiful songs. You cast a mystic spell upon us with the warmth and richness of your golden voice. Then you drifted into the night and disappeared, leaving only the enchantment of your magic melodies.

"Tonight you have come back to share with us the poetry and music of our land.

"Now it is our turn to express to you our love."

Michel stopped a moment. Then he continued with the poetry of Fair Island, which he had kept in his heart to offer to The Lady with the Golden Voice.

"Michel," she said kindly, when he had finished, "I have heard many speeches in my life, but never one from the heart of a young boy, never one as beautiful as yours."

The crowd cheered and came down to the edge of the

water, forming a semicircle in front of her balcony. Confetti colored the air, and torchlights cast excited shadows on the sand.

Suddenly the crowd was still. The Lady whispered to her crew, and the ship prepared to return to the Mainland.

As Michel bowed to The Lady with the Golden Voice, there were tears in his eyes, for he had done his best.

She looked down at him and smiled. "Hurry, Michel," she said. "Take my hand. The crew is leaving for the Mainland, but I am staying here to sing my song to you."

Then she hummed a tune to which she put these words:

"I shall watch your white-sailed ships play games
  with the sea,
While they race with the tides in frostiness of dawn,
My ears will fill with the songs of birds
And the whisper of mimosa trees."

Softly Michel echoed her song. Gently he showed her the path to Sainte Anne, and hand in hand they climbed the hill, The Lady with the Golden Voice and the Messenger of Fair Island.